Ellen Duncan; And the Proctor's Daughter

William Carleton

ESPRIOS DIGITAL PUBLISHING

ELLEN DUNCAN

and

THE PROCTOR'S DAUGHTER

By William Carleton

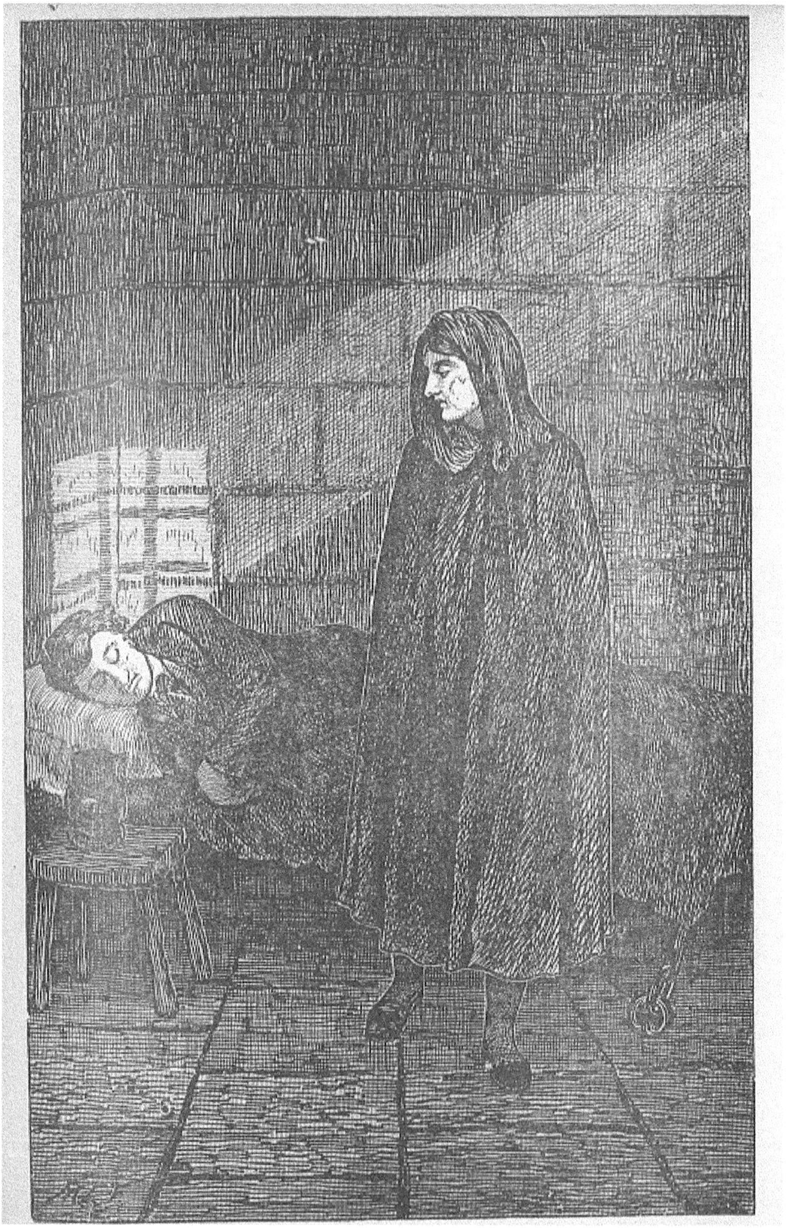

THE WORKS

OF

WILLIAM CARLETON.

VOLUME II.

JANE SINCLAIR.	THE PROCTOR'S DAUGHTER.
LHA DHU; OR, THE DARK DAY.	VATENTINE McCLUTCHY, THE IRISH AGENT
THE DEAD BOXER.	THE TITHE PROCTOR.
ELLEN DUNCAN.	THE EMIGRANTS OF AHA-DARRA.

ILLUSTRATED.

NEW YORK:
P. F. COLLIER, PUBLISHER.
1881.

CONTENTS

ELLEN DUNCAN

THE PROCTOR'S DAUGHTER

List of Illustrations

Frontispiece

One Long and Lingering Look of Affection

"Shame! Oh, for Shame!" Were the First Exclamations

ELLEN DUNCAN

There are some griefs so deep and overwhelming, that even the best exertions of friendship and sympathy are unequal to the task of soothing or dispelling them. Such was the grief of Ellen Duncan, who was silently weeping in her lone cottage on the borders of Clare—a county at that time in a frightful state of anarchy and confusion. Owen Duncan, her husband, at the period about which our tale commences, resided in the cabin where he was born and reared, and to which, as well as a few acres of land adjoining, he had succeeded on the death of his father. They had not been long married, and never were husband and wife more attached. About this time outrages began to be perpetrated; and soon increased fearfully in number. Still Owen and Ellen lived happily, and without fear, as they were too poor for the marauders to dream of getting much booty by robbing; and their religion being known to be "the ould religion ov all ov all," in a warfare that was exclusively one of party, they were more protected than otherwise. Owen never was particularly thrifty; and as his means were small, was generally embarrassed, or rather somewhat pinched in circumstances. Notwithstanding this, however, he was as happy as a king; and according to his unlettered neighbors' artless praise, "there wasn't a readier hand, nor an opener heart in the wide world—that's iv he had id—but he hadn't an' more was the pity." His entire possessions consisted of the ground we have mentioned, most part of which was so rocky as to be entirely useless—a cow, a couple of pigs, and the "the uld cabin," which consisted of four mud walls, covered with thatch, in which was an opening, "to let in the day-light, an' to let out the smoke." In the interior there was no division, or separate apartment, as the one room contained the cooking materials, and all other necessaries, beside their bed, which was placed close to the fire, and, of course, nearly under the opening in the roof. If any one spqke to Owen about the chances of rain coming down to where they slept, his universal answer was, "Shure we're naither shugar nor salt, anyhow; an' a dhrop ov or a thrifle ov wind, was niver known to do any body harm—barrin' it brought the typhus; but

God's good, an' ordhers all for the best." Owen had been brought up in this way, and so he could live by his labor, he never thought of needless luxuries; and Ellen, seeing him contented, was so herself.

For some months previous to the time of which we write, Owen's affairs had been gradually getting worse and worse; and it was with no pleasing anticipations that he looked forward to his approaching rent day. His uneasiness he studiously kept a secret from his wife, and worked away seemingly with as much cheerfulness as ever, hoping for better days, and *trusting in Providence!* However, when within a week of the time that he expected a call from the agent, he found that with all his industry he had been only able to muster five and twenty shillings, and his rent was above five pounds. So, after a good deal of painful deliberation, he thought of selling his single cow, thinking that by redoubled exertion he might after a while be enabled to repurchase her; forgetting, that before the cow was sold was really the time to make the exertion. A circumstance that greatly damped his ardor in this design was the idea of his wife's not acquiescing in it; and one evening, as they sat together by the light of the wood and turf fire, he thus opened his mind —

"Ellen, asthore, its myself that's sorry I haven't a fine large cabin, and a power o' money, to make you happier an' comfortabler than you are."

"Owen," she interrupted, "don't you know I'm very happy? an' didn't I often tell you, that it was the will of Providence that we shud be poor'? So it's sinful to be wishin' for riches."

"Bud, Ellen acushla, it's growi'n' worse wid us every day; an' I'm afeard the trouble is goin' to come on us. You know how hard the master's new agint is—how he sould Paddy Murphy's cow, an' turned him out, bekase he couldn't pay his rint; an' I'm afeard I'll have to sell *Black Bess*,' to prevint his doin' the same wid us."

"Well, Owen agra, we mustn't murmur for our disthresses; so do whatever you think right—times won't be always as they are now."

"Bud, Ellen," said he, "you're forgettin' how you'll miss the dhrop ov milk, an' the bit of fresh butter, fur whin we part wid the poor baste, you won't have even thim to comfort you."

"Indeed, an' iv I do miss them, Owen," she answered, "shure it's no matther, considherin' the bein' turned out ov one's home into the world. Remember the ould sayin' ov, 'out ov two evils always chuse the laste;' an' so, darlint, jist do whatever you think is fur the best."

After this conversation, it was agreed on by both that Owen should set out the next day but one for the town, to try and dispose of the "cow, the crathur;" and although poverty had begun to grind them a little, still they had enough to eat, and slept tranquilly. However, it so happened, that the very morning on which he had appointed to set out, *Black Bess* was seized for a long arrear of a tax that had not been either asked or paid there for some time, and driven off, with many others belonging to his neighbors, to be sold. Now you must know, good reader, that there is a feeling interwoven, as it were, in the Irish nature, that will doggedly resist anything that it conceives in the slightest or most remote degree oppressive or unjust; and that feeling then completely usurped all others in Owen's mind. He went amongst his friends, and they condoled with one another about their grievances; there was many a promise exchanged, that they would stand by each other in their future resistance to what they considered an unlawful impost. When the rent-day came, by disposing of his two pigs, and by borrowing a little, he was enabled to pay the full amount, and thus protract for some time the fear "ov bein' turned out on the world."

Some days after the whole country was in a tumult—Daly, "the procthor," was found murdered in the centre of the high road; and there was no clue perceptible, by which the perpetrators of the crime could be discovered. The very day before, Owen had borrowed the game-keeper's gun, to go, as he said, to a wild, mountainous part of the country to shoot hares; and from this circumstance, and his not having returned the day after, a strong feeling of suspicion against him was in the minds of most. In fact, on the very evening that we have represented Ellen sitting in tears, the police had come to the cabin in search of him; and their report to the magistrate was, that he had absconded. His wife was in a miserable state of mind, and her whole soul was tortured with conflicting emotions. Owen's long absence, as well as his borrowing the gun, seemed to bespeak his guilt; and yet, when she recollected the gentleness of his manner, and his hitherto blameless life, she could not deem him so, no matter how circumstances seemed against him. But then, the harrowing idea that it might be, came in to blast these newly formed hopes, and her state of suspense was one of deep and acute misery.

She was sitting, as we have said, alone; the fire, that had consisted of two or three sods of turf heaped upon the floor, had almost entirely gone out; the stools and bosses were tossed negligently here and there; and the appearance of the entire apartment was quite different from its usual neat and tidy trim. Her head was bent a little, and her hands were clasped tightly around her knees, while her body was swaying to and fro, as if the agitation of her mind would not allow of its repose. Her eyes were dry, but red from former weeping; and she was occasionally muttering, "No, he can't be guilty"—"Owen commit a murdher!—It must be an untruth!" and such like expressions. Gradually, as she thus thought aloud, her motions became more rapid, and her cheeks were no longer dry, while the light that entered through the open door becoming suddenly shaded, she turned round, and raised her tearful eyes to question the intruder. She sprang eagerly forward, and hung on his neck, (for it was Owen himself,) while she! joyfully exclaimed—

"Oh, heaven be praised, yer come back at last, to give the lie to all their reports, an' to prove yer innocence."

"Ellen, my darlint," he answered, "I knew you'd be glad to get me back," and he kissed! again and again her burning lips; "but what do you mane, acushla?—What reports! do you spake ov, an' ov what am I accused?"

"Oh, thin, Owen, I'm glad you didn't even hear ov id; an' the poliss here searchin' the house to make you pres'ner. Shure, avick, Bill Daly, the procthor, that sazed poor Black Bess, was murdhered the very mornin' you wint to shoot the hares; an' on account ov yer borryin' the gun, an' threatenin' him the day ov the sale, they said it was you that done id; but I gev thim all the lie, fur I knew you wor innocent. Now, Owen, ahagur, you look tired, sit down, an' I'll get you somethin' to ate. Och, bud I'm 'glad that yer returned safe!"

The overjoyed wife soon heaped fresh turf on the fire, and partly blowing, partly fanning it into a flame, hung a large iron pot I over it, from a hook firmly fixed in the wall. While these preparations were going forward, Owen laid aside his rough outside coat, and going to the door, looked out, as if in irresolution.

"Ellen," at length said he, turning suddenly round, "I'm thinkin' that I'd betther go to the poliss barrack an' surrindher—or rather, see what they have to say agin me; as I'm an innocent man, I've no dhread; an' if I wait till they come an' take me, it'll look as iv I was afeard."

"Thrue for you, agra," she answered; "bud it's time enough yit a bit—no one knows ov yer bein' here. You look slaved, an' had betther rest yerself, an' ate a pratee or two. I have no milk ov my own to offer you now, but I'll go an' thry an' get a dhrop from a neighbor."

When Ellen returned with a little wooden noggin full, her husband was sitting warming his hands over the fire; and it was then she recollected that he had not brought back the gun with him; besides, when she cast a glance at his clothes, they were all soiled with mud and clay, and torn in many places. But these circumstances did not for a moment operate in her mind against him, for she knew from the very manner of his first question, and the innocence of his exclamation, that the accusations and suspicions were all false. Even though he had not attempted to explain the cause of his protracted absence, she felt conscious that it was not guilt, and forbore to ask any question about it. It was he first opened the subject, as they sat together over their frugal meal.

"Ellen," said he, "sence I saw you last, I wint through a dale ov hardship; an' I little thought, on my return, that I'd be accused ov so black a crime."

"Och, shure enough, Owen darlint; but I hope it 'ill be all for the best. I little thought I'd see the day that you'd be suspected ov murdher."

"Well, Ellen aroon, all's in it is, it can't be helped. Bud as I was sayin'—whin I left this, I cut acrass by Sheemus Doyle's, an' so up into the mountain, where I knew the hares were coorsin' about in plenty. I shot two or three ov thim; an' as night began to fall, I was thinkin' ov comin' home, whin I heerd the barkin' ov a dog a little farther up, in the wild part, where I never ventured afore. I dunna what prompted me to folly id bud, any how, I did, an' wint on farther an' farther. Well, Ellen agra, I at last come to a deep valley, full up a'most of furze an' brambles, an' I seen a black thing runnin' down the edge ov id. It was so far off, I thought it was a hare, an' so I lets fly, an' it rowled over an' over. Whin I dhrew near, what was it bud a purty black spaniel; an' you may be shure I was sorry for shootin' it, an' makin' such a mistake. I lays down the gun, an' takes id in my arms, an' the poor crathur licked the hand that shot id. Thin suddenly there comes up three sthrange min, an' sazin' me as if I wor a child, they carrid me down wid them, cursin' an' abusin' me all the way. As they made me take a solemn oath not to revale what I saw there, I can't tell you any more: but they thrated me badly, an' it was only yesterday I escaped."

"Well, Owen, ahagur, we ought to be thankful that you're back here safe; bud do you think the magisthrate will be satisfied with this story—they are always anxious to do justice, but they must be satisfied."

"In throth, they are, machree: but shure I'll sware to id; an', besides, you know, the raal murdherer may be discovered—for God never lets it, ov all other crimes, go athout punishment. An' now I'll just go to the barracks at onst, an' be out ov suspinse."

Ere Duncan had concluded his sentence, the tramp of feet was heard outside, and in a few seconds the cabin was full of armed men, who came to take him prisoner. He had been seen entering his cabin; and they immediately, as soon as they could muster a party, set out to make him captive. As he was known to most of them, and did not make the slightest attempt at resistance, they treated him gently, but bound his hands firmly behind his back, and took every necessary precaution. Though Ellen, while it seemed at a distance, had conversed calmly about his surrender, she was violently agitated at the appearance of the armed force. She clung to her husband's knees, and refused to part with him, wildly screaming, "He's innocent! My husband's innocent!" and when all was prepared, she walked by his side to the magistrate's house, (a distance of three miles,) her choking sobs and burning tears attesting the violence of her uncontrolled feelings. A short examination was gone through there; and the circumstantial evidence that was adduced made the case look very serious. One man positively swore, that he had seen Duncan pass by in the morning, in the direction where the body was found, and that he was armed with a gun. Another, that in about an hour afterwards he had heard a shot, but supposed it was some person coursing, and that the report was just where the body was found, and where Owen had been seen proceeding to. His only cow having been seized by Daly, a threat that he was heard uttering, and his absence from home, was duly commented on; and finally, he was committed to prison to abide his trial at the Ennis Assizes. While all this was going forward, Ellen's emotions were most agonizing. She stared wildly at the magistrate and the two witnesses; and as the evidence was proceeded with, she sometimes hastily put back her hair, as if she thought she was under the influence of a dream. But when his final committal was made out, and her mind glanced rapidly at the concurrent testimony, and the danger of Owen, she rushed forward, and flinging her arms round him, wildly exclaimed—

"They shan't part us—they shan't tear us asunder! No, no, Owen, I will go wid you to presson! Oh, is id come to this wid us?—You to be dhragged from home, accused of murdher—and I—I—Father of marcies, keep me in my sinses—I'm goin' mad—wild, wild mad!"

"Ellen!" said Owen, gently unwinding her arms, and kissing her forehead, while a scalding tear fell from his eye on her cheek— "Ellen, asthore machree! don't be overcome. There's a good girl, dhry yer eyes. That God that knows I'm guiltless, 'ill bring me safe through all. May his blessin' be on you, my poor colleen, till we meet agin! You know you can come an' see me. Heaven purtect you, Ellen, alanna!—Heaven purtect you!"

When he was finally removed, she seemed to lose all power, and but for the arm of a bystander would have fallen to the ground. It was not without assistance that she was at length enabled to reach her cabin.

It is strange how man's feelings and powers are swayed by outward circumstances, and how his pride and strength may be entirely overcome by disheartening appearances! So it was with Owen: although constantly visited in prison by his faithful wife—although conscious of his own innocence—and although daily receiving assurances of hope from a numerous circle of friends—yet still his spirit drooped; the gloom of imprisonment, the idea of danger, the ignominy of public execution and all the horrors of innocent conviction, gradually wore away his mental strength; and when the assize time approached, he was but a thin shadow of the former bluff, healthy Owen Duncan. In so short a time as this, can care and harrowing thought exercise its influence on the human frame!

Never was there a finer or more heavenly morning than that which ushered in the day of trial. The court-house was crowded to suffocation, the mob outside fearfully numerous, and never before, perhaps, was Ennis in such a state of feverish excitement. Daly's murder was as nought in the minds of all, in comparison with Duncan's accusation. Alas! the former was an occurrence of too frequent repetition, to be very much thought of; but the latter—namely, Owen's being suspected—was a subject of the extremest wonder. His former high character—his sobriety—his quietness, and his being a native of the town, in some measure accounted for this latter feeling; and there was an inward conviction in most men's minds, that he was guiltless of the crime for which he was accused. Although the court-house was crowded, yet when the prisoner was called to the bar, a pin could be heard to drop in any part of the place. There was a single female figure leaning on the arm of an aged and silver-haired, though hale and healthy countryman, within a few feet of the dock; and as the prisoner advanced, and laying his hand on the iron railing, confronted the judges and the court, she slowly raised the hood of the cloak, in which she was completely muffled, and gazed long and earnestly on his face. There was in that wistful look, a fear—a hope—an undying tenderness; and when his eye met hers, there was a proud, yet soft and warm expression in its glance, that reassured her sinking heart. As she looked round on the court, and the many strange faces, and all the striking paraphernalia of justice, a slight shudder crept silently over her frame, and she clung closer to her companion, as if to ask for all the protection he could afford. It was Ellen and her father who came, the former summoned as a witness, and the latter to accompany and support the daughter of his aged heart.

Duncan was arraigned: and on being asked the usual question of "guilty, or not guilty?" he answered in a clear, calm voice, "Not guilty, my Lord!" and the trial proceeded. The same evidence that was given at the magistrate's house was a second time repeated; and, evidently, its train of circumstances made a deep impression on the court. While the first part of the examination was going forward, Ellen remained as motionless as a statue, scarcely daring to move or breathe; but when the depositions went more and more against Owen, her respirations became quick, short, and gaspish; and when the crier desired her to get up on the table, it was with difficulty that she obeyed him. When seated, she gazed timidly round on the crowd of counsellors and the judges, as though to bespeak their sympathy; but then, not meeting a single glance from which to glean even the shadow of hope, she covered her face with her hands. A moment or two elapsed, and she grew more assured, and the counsel for the Crown proceeded with the examination.

"Ellen Duncan, is not that your name?" was the first question.

"It is, Sir," she shrinkingly answered, without raising her eyes.

"Do you know the prisoner at the bar?"

"Do I know the pres'ner at the bar?" she reiterated; "do I know Owen Duncan? Shure, isn't he my husband?"

"Do you recollect the night of the twenty-first of September?"

"I do, Sir."

"Can you swear to whether your husband was at home on that night or not?"

Her voice faltered a little as she answered in the negative; and on the presiding judge repeating the question, with the addition of, "Did he return at all next day?" it seemed as if she first thought that her answers might criminate him still farther, and clasping her I hands convulsively together, and raising her face to the bench, while the scalding tears chased each other down her sunken cheek, she passionately exclaimed—

"Oh, for the love of heaven, don't ask me any thing that 'ill be worse for him! Don't, counsellor jewel, don't! don't ask me to swear any thing that 'ill do him harm; for I can't know what I'm sayin' now, as the heart within me is growin' wake."

After a few cheering expressions from the bench, who evidently were much moved by her simply energetic language and action, she was asked whether she could tell the Court where her husband spent that and the following nights; and with all the eagerness that an instantaneously formed idea of serving him could give, she answered—

"Oh, yis! yis! my Lord, I can. He was in the mountains shootin' wid Phil Doran's gun, an' he was sazed by some men, that made him stop wid thim, an' take an oath not to revale who they wor, an' they thrated him badly; so afther three days he made his escape, and come home to the cabin, whin he was taken by the poliss."

"One word more, an' you may go down—What was done with that gun?"

The judge's hard and unmoved tone of voice seemed to bring misgiving to her mind, and she trembled from head to foot as she falteringly answered—

"The wild boys of the mountain kep' it, my Lord, an' so he couldn't bring id home wid him. But, indeed, my Lord, indeed he's innocent—I'll swear he never done it! Fur, oh! iv you knew the tindherness ov his heart—he that niver hurt a fly! Don't be hard on him for the love ov mercy, an' I'll pray for you night an' day."

This was the last question she was asked, and having left the table, and regained her former position by her father's side, she listened with moveless, motionless intensity to the judge's "charge." He recapitulated the evidence—dwelt on the strong circumstances that seemed to bespeak his guilt—spoke of the mournful increase of crime—of laws, and life, and property being at stake—and finally closed his address with a sentence expressive of the extreme improbability of the prisoner's defence; for he, on being asked if he had any thing further to say, replied in the negative, only asserting, in the most solemn manner, his innocence of the charge.

The jury retired, and Ellen's hard, short breathings, alone told that she existed. Her head was thrown back, her lips apart, and slightly quivering, and her eyes fixedly gazing on the empty box, with an anxious and wild stare of hope and suspense. Owen's face was very pale, and his lips livid—there was the slightest perceptible emotion about the muscles of his mouth, but his eye quailed not, and his broad brow had the impress of an unquenched spirit as firmly fixed as ever on its marble front. A quarter of an hour elapsed, and still the same agonizing suspense—another, and the jury returned not—five minutes, and they reentered. Ellen's heart, beat as if it would burst her bosom; and Owen's pale cheek became a little more flushed, and his eye full of anxiety. The foreman in a measured, feelingless tone pronounced the word "Guilty!" and a thrill of horror passed through the entire court, while that sickness which agonizes the very depths of the soul convulsed Owen's face with a momentary spasm, and he faltered "God's will be done." The judge slowly drew on the black cap, and still Ellen moved not—it seemed as if the very blood within her veins was frozen, and that her life's pulses no more could execute their functions. No man, however brave or hardened, can view the near approach of certain death, and be unmoved; and as that old man, in tremulous tones, uttered the dread fiat of his fate, Owen's eyes seemed actually to sink within his head—the veins of his brow swelled and grew black, and his hands grasped the iron rail that surrounded the dock, as though he would force his fingers through it. When all was over, and the fearful cap drawn off, Ellen seemed only then to awake to consciousness. Her eyes slowly opened to their fullest extent—their expression of despair was absolutely frightful—a low, gurgling, half-choking sob forced itself from between her lips, and ere a hand could be outstretched to save her, she fell, as if quickly dashed to the ground by no mortal power—her piercing shriek of agony ringing through the court-house, with a fearful, prolonged cadence.

Evening approached, and the busy crowd of idlers had passed away, some to brood over what they had seen, and others to forget, in the bustle of life, that there were woes and miseries in the hearts of their fellow-beings. Owen was remanded to prison, as his execution was not to take place till the commission was over, thus giving him more than a week to prepare for that final doom. The light that struggled through the bars of his cell rested fully on the stooping figure of his wife, as she bent over the rude bed on which he lay; and her hot tears fell fast down her cheeks, as she thought how soon they were doomed to part for ever. Hope was not, however, entirely dead within her, for the jury had strongly recommended him to mercy;

Ellen Duncan; And the Proctor's Daughter

and ignorant as she was of forms and ceremonies—helpless as a lone woman in misfortune always is—she had determined on going to Dublin, to kneel at the feet of the Lord Lieutenant—then the proud and whimsical Duke of ———, and there to solicit his pardon. Having hesitated for some time as to the manner in which she should break it to him, and ask his advice, she thus began—

"Owen, dear Owen! do you know what I've been thinkin' ov, an' where I've been thinkin' ov goin'?"

There was no answer returned for some time, and on looking at him more earnestly, she was astonished to find that he had sank into a profound slumber. "Guilt," thought she, "is not there!" and her resolution was taken instantly—she would not wake him—she would not let him know her purpose—and if she succeeded, her eyes flashed through her tears at the anticipation of his rapturous surprise. Stooping lower, she gently pressed her lips to his; and kneeling beside his bed, poured forth a short but fervent prayer to Him in whom alone we can put our trust—"In whose hand is the soul of every living-thing, and the breath of all mankind"—"Who preserveth not the life of the wicked, but giveth right to the poor." There was something exceedingly and touchingly beautiful in the attitude of that young wife—her hands clasped, her lips moving with her prayer, like rose-leaves with the evening breeze, and her upturned face, with its holy and deep religious expression. Having concluded her fervent petition, she noiselessly arose, and giving her sleeping husband one long and lingering look of affection, that death could not estrange, she silently glided from the cell.

On the third night from the events which we have narrated, a poor woman was observed wending her toilsome way through the streets of the metropolis. Her appearance bespoke fatigue and long travel; and as she neared the Upper Castle gate, she had to lean against the railing for support. The lamps were lighted, carriages rolling to and fro, and all the buzz of life was ringing in her ears; but, oh! from the expression of pain and suffering in her face, and the shrinking with which she surveyed the sentinels pacing up and down, it was evident that her mind but little accorded with the scenes by which she was surrounded. She slowly and fearfully entered the wide court-yard—a flood of light was streaming from the windows of the vice-regal dwelling, and a crowd of idlers stood around about, viewing the entrance of the visitors, for it appeared as if there were a revel of some kind going on. Ellen's heart sank within her, as she heard the carriages rolling and dashing across the pavement, for she felt that amid the bustle of company and splendor her poor appeal might be entirely unnoticed. As she waited, she saw several of the persons assembled thrust; rudely back by the soldiers that were on guard, and when she advanced a step or two for the purpose of entering, a brute in human shaped pushed her with a blow of the end of his musket back against the pillar. He was about to repeat his violence, when the poor creature fell on her knees before him and screamed—

"Sojer darlin', don't stop me! I'm only goin' in to plade fur my husband's life, an shure you wont prevent me? I've traveled many a wairy mile to get here in time; an' oh! fur marcy's sake let me pass."

At this moment the carriage of the eccentric and beautiful Lady ——, one of the wildest, strangest, and best-hearted females of the Irish Court, set down its lovely burden. She had seen the whole transaction of the sentinel, and heard Ellen's pathetic appeal, and her heart was instantly moved in her favor, for the example of fashion had not yet frozen up its finer feelings. Partly through the workings of a softened heart, and partly to make what was then all the rage, a scene or sensation, she resolved instantly to get her admitted to the presence of the Duke—nay, to present her herself. She was well known to be a favorite, and whatever whim of hers took place, no matter how extravagant, was sure to meet his hearty concurrence. She desired Ellen to rise and follow her; and the poor creature's eyes streamed with tears as she invoked a fervent blessing on the head of her lovely protectress. While passing up the grand staircase, amid the wondering gaze and suppressed titter of many a pampered menial, she instructed her how to proceed; and having received a hasty account of all, and desired her not to be faint-hearted, she turned to the simpering master of ceremonies to tell him of her "dear delightful freak;" there was a glad smile on her lip, and a glowing crimson on her cheek, but still there was a glistening moisture in her fine eyes, that told of soft and womanish feeling.

The Duke was sitting on a chair of crimson velvet; a cushion of the same costly material supported his feet; and he was looking with an appearance of apathy and ennui on the splendid group around him. The glitter of the lights, the lustre of the jewels, and the graceful waving of the many-colored plumes, gave every thing a courtly, sumptuous appearance, and the air was heavy with odors, the fragrant offering of many a costly exotic. Suddenly every eye was turned on the door with, wonder and astonishment, and every voice was hushed as Lady ——— entered, her cheeks blushing from excitement, and her eye bright with anticipated triumph. She led the poor and humbly clad Ellen by the hand, who dared not look up, but with her gaze riveted on the splendid carpet, was brought like an automaton to the feet of the Duke, where she mechanically knelt down.

"Will yer Excillincy be plazed," began Lady ———, playfully mimicking the brogue, "to hear this poor crathur's complaint. Her husband has been condimned to die for a murdher he didn't commit by no manner ov manes, as the sayin' is; an' as there was a sthrong recommindation to marcy, if you'll grant him a reprieve, you'll have all our prayers, and (in an under tone) your Excillincy knows you want thim?"

The Duke seemed a little bewildered, as if he could not make out what it meant, and the glittering crowd now surrounded the group; when Ellen, who had ventured to look timidly up, conceived that the Duke hesitated about the pardon, (poor creature! she little knew that he had not even heard of Owen's trial,) eagerly grasped the drapery of his chair, and while the big tears rolled from beneath her eyelids, exclaimed—

"Oh! may the great and just Providence, that sees the workin' ov all our hearts, pour a blessin' on yer Lordship's head—may His holy grace be wid you for iver an' iver, an' do listen to my prayers! My husband is innocent—an' oh! as you hope for marcy at thee last day, be merciful now him."

"Lady ———," said the Duke, "what is the meaning of all this—will you explain?"

"Your Excellency," answered she, in the natural sweet pathos of her tones, "it is a poor man who has been condemned to die on circumstantial evidence. He has been strongly recommended to mercy, and this, weeping female is his wife, I found her outside praying for admission, and have brought her hither. She has traveled mostly on foot upwards of ninety miles to I ask a pardon; and I trust you will not refuse a reprieve, till your Grace has time to; inquire into the circumstance. 'This is the head and front of my offending.'"

"May heaven bless yer Ladyship," burst from the depths of Ellen's grateful heart, "fur befriendin' thim that had no support but his gracious marcy."

Lady ———'s suit was eagerly seconded by many a fair creature, who thronged around; and the Duke smiled, as he answered,

"Well, well! one could not refuse so many fair beseechers, so we will order him to be reprieved. And there, now, let the poor woman be removed."

Ellen's heart was light, and her eye was glad, and her very inmost soul was thankful to the Omnipotent, as she that night rested for a. few hours, ere she set out on her return; and Lady ———, as she pressed her costly pillow, felt a fuller sense of happiness in being useful to her fellow-creature than ever she experienced before. Oh! that all the wealthy and in power were incited by similar feelings. The remainder of our simple tale is soon told. The reprieve arrived—the sentence was changed to banishment—and the very day appointed for Owen's death was that of his wife's successful return. One week previous to the embarkation of those sentenced to transportation, a man was to be executed for sheep-stealing. On the drop he confessed his guilt, and that he, and not Duncan, was the murderer of Daly. Owen was immediately released, and a subscription raised for him, with which, as well as with a weighty purse presented to Ellen by Lady ———, he took a comfortable farm, and rebought "Black Bess."

THE PROCTOR'S DAUGHTER

"Huroo! at id agin. Success, Briney. Ha! take that, you ould dust. Will you bewitch our cattle now, Nanny? Whoo—ha, ha, ha!—at id agin, boys—that's your sort."

Such were a few of the explosives of mingled fun and devilment that proceeded from a group of ragged urchins, who were busily employed in pelting with hard mud, sods and other missiles, an old and decrepit woman, whose gray hair and infirmities ought to have been her protection, but whose reputation as an evil disposed witch proved quite the contrary. Nanny, for such was her name, was leaning, or rather sitting, against a bank at the road side, shaking occasionally her crutch at her tormentors, and muttering a heavy curse as missile after missile fell thickly around her. The shouts of laughter proceeding from the annoying children, as she tried in vain to rise, and impotently threatened, made her imprecations come doubly bitter; but her eye was never wet, nor did she once even by a look appeal to their pity. Her figure was bent with age, and her shaking hands brown and fleshless—her hair was gray and wiry, and escaped from beneath her cap, in short, thin, tangled masses—her eyes were dark and deep set, and her lips and mouth had fallen in as her teeth had gradually decayed. She was clad in a russet gown, much the worse for the wear, and a scarlet cloak, or rather a cloak that had once been scarlet, but was now completely faded from its original color. It had been broken here and there, but was pieced with different colored cloths, so as to appear a motley and strange garment; and her bony feet were bare and unprotected. Nanny, from different circumstances, was unanimously elected the witch or bugbear of the village; and though the brats were then so busy annoying her, at night, or in a lonesome place, they would fly like lightning even at her approach; and some of them actually trembled while shouting, though they did not like to exhibit their fear to their companions. In the first place, she lived completely alone in a hovel on the mountain side, where, save heath, rock, and fern, there was not a single thing on which the eye could rest; then, no one knew from whence she came, and lights were frequently seen shining through her unglazed windows at hours when spirits were supposed to be abroad; besides, more than once a group of dark figures had been observed standing at twilight near her door, and were always set down as ministering demons, awaiting the pleasure of their mistress. Whenever a cow ceased giving milk—whenever a lamb or pig got any disease and died—it was unanimously attributed to the spite and venom of "Nanny the witch;" in fact, no human being could be viewed, with more mingled feelings of fear and hate than she was by all the inhabitants of the village. The boys still continued their unfeeling attack; and she now was silent and gloomy, and did not menace nor even mutter a curse, but her firmness had not left her, for her brow was darkly bent, and her small black eyes emitted a flash of wild though concentrated anger and revenge. Nor did those who passed from time to time, by word or gesture discourage the young urchins from their attack; sometimes they even stood looking complacently on, wondering at the reckless courage of the boys, as they would not for worlds dare to rise a hand against one so very powerful. Suddenly a louder whoop than any they had yet given, told that they had just invented some new mode of annoyance, and a short, hard-featured, red-headed boy, whom they called Briney, ran whooping and hallooing towards them, bearing a large hairy cap, which he triumphantly declared was full of rotten eggs—those delicious affairs which smash so delightfully off an unprotected face, and which used to be in great demand when pillories were in fashion.

"I must have first shot!" roared Briney, as he placed his burden down in the midst, and seized one of the eggs it contained.

"Sorra a bit, Briney!" screamed another, striding before him—"I've a betther aim nor you."

"You a betther aim!" scornfully retorted he; "thry id:" and his hand was upraised in the act of pelting, but was as suddenly stopped and withheld, as a pretty, tiny, fair-haired child, tripped forward from an opposite stile; and perceiving what was going on, ran quickly to the old woman, and laying down a pitcher that she bore, stood before her, facing the crowd of boys, her mild, soft blue eye flashing displeasure, and her cheeks flushed with a deep pink suffusion.

"Shame! oh, for shame!" were the first exclamations that escaped her, and her sweet voice trembled with anger.

"Bedad, it's purty Minny herself, sure enough!" muttered one urchin to another, as they hesitated what to do, each evidently unwilling to encounter the reproaches they were sure of receiving; and one or two scampered off the instant she spoke.

Then turning round to the old woman, and perceiving that her lips looked dry and parched, she ran to the pitcher, and lifting it to her mouth with much softness and compassion, exclaimed,

"Poor Nanny, you look dhry, an' here's some wather. Take a little sup, an' it 'ill revive you! Oh; if I wor here a little bit sooner."

Nanny raised her eyes to thank her, and did as she requested; and it was indeed a touching thing to see that child in all the budding beauty of infancy, attending so anxiously on the withered female, whose name was seldom pronounced without dread or malediction. The urchins looked on for some time with open mouths and staring eyes; and then, headed by Briney, giving a farewell shout, to show they were not entirely disconcerted, bravely took to their heels.

"May the blessins ov the poor and persecuted folly on yer path, my purty child!" gratefully exclaimed the old woman, as her eyes rested on the cherub face and infantine figure of her protectress, and they now were dewy and wet with tears.

"Shall I help you to rise, Nanny?" asked she, her little heart dancing with pleasure at hearing the fervent wish: "iv you like to go home, an' you think me sthrong enough, I'll help you on!"

"From my heart I thank you, my purty golden haired child," said the old woman, as with her assistance she at length stood up; "bud you seem to know who I am, and I wondher yer not afeard ov me. Minny, I think they called you—who is the happy father ov my little darlin'?"

"I'm Minny Whelan," gently answered the little girl; upon which Nanny shrunk hastily back, and a fearful change overspread her features.

"Minny Whelan!—you the proctor's daughter? Those smiling lips—those tinder, soft eyes—that rich yellow hair—an' that warm an' feelin' heart, Minny Whelan's. Oh, it can't, it mustn't be—I won't believe id!"

The little girl laughed, although wonder lurked in her eye, and repeated innocently,

"Sure enough, I am the procthor's daughter: bud you don't hate me for id—do you?

"Come close to me, child, till I look upon you," said Nanny, in a cold and altered tone of voice; and then, as Minny fearlessly advanced, she laid her aged hands on her head, and pushing back the profusion of her curling hair, looked long and anxiously on her. A hot tear fell upon the child's forehead as she withdrew her hand; and in a broken, voice the old woman exclaimed,

"You are—you are indeed his child; bud have naither his black look, nor his hard an' baneful heart—so—so—I cannot hate you! For years I've never met with kindness, till you wor kind. Minny, heaven 'ill reward; you for id; an' may its blessin' be wid you, is the prayer ov your father's bittherest foe!"

At this the child hesitated for an instant, as if she did not comprehend the latter part of Nanny's sentence; and then innocently taking her hand, she looked up to her face and said—

"Bud maybe yer too tired to go home now all the ways, Nanny, so iv you'll come home wid me, I'm sure my father won't be angry, an' will"—

"Go home wid you!" wildly reiterated the old woman, her eyes blazing so fearfully, that the child shrunk instinctively back—"crass your father's flure!—inther the man's house who sint my son—my only son!—my heart's blood!—from his native land, wid disgrace upon his name, and the heavy hand ov power crushin' him to the earth! Never!—these eyes, that once could laugh wid happiness, will burn in their sockets first, and this withered heart, once so warm and joyful, will burst afore I ever think ov id!"

"Nanny," tremblingly said Minny, "you spake so wild you make me afeard—I hope I haven't done anything to vex you!"

"You! Oh! no, no—you force me to love you! I couldn't hate you, although yer father—bud no matther. Minny, good bye—may the Almighty guard you."

Ellen Duncan; And the Proctor's Daughter

The day passed away as Summer days are wont, in softness and languor, and the sun descended in gold and crimson, leaving a bright halo in the west to mark his resting place. Night came on serene and still, and the quiet moon ascended her heavenly throne, while the refreshing dews fell upon the flowers, whose leaves opened to receive them, parched, as they were with the burning lustre of the mid-day sun. Midnight had already passed; and all was as silent as if no living or created thing existed upon the earth to mar its splendid beauty with the wild indulgence of its fiercer passions. A strong light was gleaming from the interior of Nanny's cabin, which we have already said was situated on the mountain side; and the noisy sounds of revelry were heard proceeding from within. Could any of the superstitious have summoned courage to approach sufficiently near, and listen for a moment, the idea of spirits would soon be dissipated in the bluff, hoarse voices which were laughing and grumbling, and singing, sometimes alternately, and sometimes all together. But we had better introduce the reader to the interior, and then he will be a better judge of the nature of the orgies carried on.

The cabin consisted of but one small apartment, in the centre of which blazed a, huge fire (summer though it was) of dried peat. The smoke sought egress where it might, but still left a sufficient canopy over the heads of the occupants, as completely to hide the dingy and charred rafters, and did not seem in the slightest degree to annoy the optical powers of any one, so accustomed where they to this kind of atmosphere. Round this fire about ten were seated or squatted down, and were all at the time busily employed in some noisy and apparently angry disputation. However, this did not prevent the bottle from being freely passed amongst them; and so cordial were they in embracing it, that Nanny, who sat a little apart, was often called on to replenish it with mountain-dew. On a table or dresser that stood by the wall, were three or four large pistols, besides an old sword or two, and a few rusted bayonets: piled against it were two large muskets, evidently kept with more care than the rest of the arms, for they were brightly polished, and looked even new. A couple of powder-horns, a tin box containing shot and bullets, and a large iron mallet, used in breaking open doors, completed the array, which could leave no doubt as to the men who occupied the cabin.

Ellen Duncan; And the Proctor's Daughter

"Come, Nanny acushla, give us another dhrop of that you gev us last," exclaimed one, whose rolling eyes gave token, of approaching intoxication; "you're not used to be sparin', an' considherin' the way you get id, needn't be so—eh? Dick, what do you say to another drink?"

"Game to the last," answered the man addressed—"never refuse id."

"Why, Nanny," observed a low but muscularly formed man, who seemed from his manner to exercise some slight command amongst his associates, "what's the matther wid you to-night? Sure we're goin' to do what you've long been axin' us, an' what you first gev us lave to meet here for—an' by doin' so we've got the fame of bein' not quite right. The villain of a procthor that suit poor Bob off afore he could look about him, 'ill resave his pay to-night, anyhow. What say you, boys?"

"No doubt ov it!—All right!—Whoo! sartinly!" they grumbled and shouted in reply; and then, the whiskey having been brought, the health of Nanny's absent son, and their companion, was loudly proposed and drank.

"I say, Dick," hiccupped the first speaker, who now began to wax drunk, "what is your op—op—opinion should, we do to ould Whelan? You know, I'm (hiccup) not natherally crule, bud suppose (hiccup) we jist cut the ears off the baste, an' (hiccup) lave him hard ov hearin' for the rest ov his life!"

"I'm not the man to disagree wid a rasonable iday," ironically answered Dick.

"What do you say to that, my ould (hiccup) woman?" again asked he, addressing Nanny, who had drawn near to listen; "suppose we sarve him that-a-way, will you be (hiccup) satisfied; or maybe you'd sooner we'd prevint his bein' annoyed wid a cough by (hiccup) cuttin' his informin' throat!"

While he spoke, an indescribable expression lighted up the old woman's eye, and she stood a moment, as if a struggle was going on between long-brooded-over revenge and some newly awakened sympathy. The rest of the men were busy with other schemes, and did not even hear the last conversation, for they had before agreed to pay Whelan a visit that night, and Nanny had eagerly entered into their intentions; for she had an only son, who, being wild and dissipated, had got connected with the very gang at present in her cabin, and through Whelan's means (he having informed against him) was transported. An Irish mother soon looks upon the faults of a darling child with levity: and when he was torn from her arms, in the madness of grief she had vowed vengeance against Whelan; and though he soon after removed to where he then was, she followed him, and took up her residence on the mountain, where, as she was a stranger, and had no apparent means of living, a report of her communion with evil spirits was soon spread abroad. This she rather encouraged than otherwise, by the advice of the men whom she fixed on as the completers of her revenge, and by such means the lights and nightly noises were placed to the account of anything but their real cause.

She had endured many griefs, and many mortifications, from her reputation as a witch, but met every thing in that way with patience, as the dream of her soul was revenge, and that dream by such means alone could be realized. However, when on the very point of its completion, one of those sudden and mysterious changes which often takes place in the human mind made her waver in her purpose; and the child of her intended victim having behaved so tenderly and so kindly when all the rest hooted at and tormented her, made her fervently wish that she could turn the fierce men around her from that fell purpose which she herself had nourished till it grew into a fixed, and, she dreaded, an unalterable determination.

"Hadn't yez betther wait," she tremblingly began, scarcely knowing what she was about to propose—"another night 'ill do as well for Whelan."

"How's this," interrupted one of them, "Nanny, you growing lukewarm!—you proposin' another night—are you beginnin' to be afeard we'll be hindhered from payin' him off, or are you repentin' yer former anxious desire?"

"No—no!" hastily answered she, dreading lest they should discover her feelings, as she well knew that many amongst them had revenge to be gratified as well as herself; "I don't repine as regards him, bud—bud—his daughter—poor little Manny—the purty goolden-haired child!—I wouldn't like any thing 'ud harm her, an' I'm afeard ov her bein' hurted—that's all."

"He did not feel so six years ago," said a deep voice at her elbow, "whin yer only son was sint off from home an' counthry through his manes!"

Nanny started, she knew not why, at the tones of the speaker, and turned round to look closer at him; but his back was towards her, and a large loose coat prevented all recognition of his person; besides, bringing an occasional newly enrolled stranger there, was a common circumstance, so she soon forgot the momentary surprise she had met in her anxiety about their intention.

"He is a brute—his heart is harder nor steel, an' he must be punished," said another, whose bent brow and flashing black eye spoke of malignity and crime.

"But his child—his poor little Minny!" exclaimed Nanny, "sure you wouldn't injure her—she hasn't deserved id at yer hands—she has done nothin', but is a sweet an' kind-hearted crathur. Oh! iv you had seen her whin I was in the village, an' the boys were hootin' an' peltin' me, an' no one interfered to protect the hated Nanny—iv you had seen the little angel how she stood before me, an' cried out 'shame!' an' held up the pitcher for me to dhrink, an' helped me to rise, offerin' me the shelter of her father's house, little dhramin' ov whom she was spakin' to—you wouldn't have a thought ov hurtin' her—bud—no one—no one could harm Minny!—she is too sweet, too pure, too like a little angel!"

"A hair of the child's head shall not be touched!" said the same deep voice that had before made Nanny start; "bud he, the informher an' the prosecuthor, must feel our vengeance!"

Nanny was silent—she saw that further parley was useless, and was obliged to bear with the concession she had already obtained. Meanwhile, the men having ascertained that it was time they were stirring, hastily equipped themselves, and prepared to start. When. they were leaving the house, the stranger, whose voice had so startled her, took her hand, and though his face was studiously averted, she heard him say solemnly'—

"Nanny, good bye!—my promise I'll keep sacred—the good child shall not be touched!"

She had not time to utter her thanks, for his hand as hastily relinquished its hold, and ere she could speak, all were gone, and she heard the buzz of their voices, as in a group they descended the mountain.

The bright moonbeams silvered the motionless leaves of the trees that surrounded Whelan's cottage—there was not a stir within—no light gleamed from the lattice, and the small thin brook that bubbled through the long grass a little in its front, seemed to hush its merry song to a mere low trickling sound, as if in unison with the universal repose. A dark group of figures stood in the little garden before the door, as if debating how they should act. Two of them, separated a little from the rest, conferred together, one of whom was the stranger we have already noticed, and the other the man we have spoken of as seeming to possess some command over them all. Suddenly the latter started, and exclaimed in the quick, sharp tone of command—

"Advance, men, an' smash the door—there's no use in delayin' longer."

An almost instantaneous crash was the answer, and the door flew from its hinges, and four or five of the men rushed into the cottage, while the rest kept watch outside. Exclamations of surprise, mingled with harsh, epithets, were heard within; and then they appeared a second time, dragging with them the unfortunate and trembling owner, whom they had just torn from his bed. A loud shout from the rest spoke their eagerness for his punishinent; and amidst prayers for mercy, and entreaties, he was dragged to the centre of the garden, placed on his knees; and his hands firmly tied behind his back.

"Now, Misther Whelan, *acushla*," asked! one, in a jeering tone, "would you be jist pleased to make yer choice between two purty little invintions of ours—*cardin* an *ear-ticklin'*."

The poor man trembled violently, and his livid lips opened but he could not utter a word.

"What an obstinate, silent ould baste you are," said the same man, "not to give a civil answer to my question. Bud maybe the look o' this plaything id drive spake outov you—oh, you may stare now!" Saying this, he drew forth a board with a thick handle, the bottom part of which was closely studded with nails and sharp pieces of iron, in imitation of the cards they use for wool, and continued— "Would you admire the taste of this in the flesh on your back, my informin' codger!—eh?"

Upon this, shouts of "card him! card him!" arose from the group, and his hands were quickly unloosed, and he was violently dashed on his face, while some held his legs and others his arms. Then his back was stripped, and the stranger laid the board flatly on it, with the iron points touching the flesh, while another stood up with the large mallet ready to drive them in, the shrieks of the victim becoming more and more faint. Just as the man who held the weapon last named was about to strike, and just as a demon grin of satisfied vengeance distorted the otherwise handsome features of the stranger, a light and tiny form flew screaming towards them, her long yellow hair floating in the night-breeze, and her white dress hanging loosely about her delicate limbs. It was Minny, who, unmindful of all, and seeing only her father, threw herself on her knees beside him, exclaiming in tones of agony:

"Oh, my father—my dear father—what is the matter?—what are they goin' to do wid you?"

The stranger started at the tones of her voice, and on gazing at her for a moment, flung the card to a distance, and catching her in his arms, kissed away the tears which covered her cheeks, as she struggled for release.

"Is it you," he said with much emotion, "that I promised to purtect?—You, who succored an' saved me when I was dyin' for want? An' are you the daughter ov Whelan the procthor?"

The men, perplexed at the apparition of the child, mechanically had released their prisoner; and he, starting up with the sudden hope of freedom, stood confronting the stranger, who yet held his child.

"Gracious Providence!" he exclaimed in wonder, as the moonlight streamed on the face he was trying to recognize—"Is id—can id be Robert Dillon?"

"Yis, Whelan!" was the answer, "it is the man you name—the man you caused to be thried an' banished, an' the man who came here to have revange!"

"Oh. don't hurt him—don't hurt him—he is *my* father," cried the little Minny who now also seemed to recognize him.

"Iv he was surrounded wid fiends," answered Dillon, kissing her fair smooth brow, "iv he was for ever on the watch, I'd still have my revenge: bud for your sake, sweet, good-natured child—for your sake, I'll not allow him to be touched!"

A murmur here began to rise among some of the men, while the leader, with one or two others, seemed to take part with the returned son of Nanny Dillon. Upon this he added—

"I was weary an' wake wid fatigue an' hunger—I couldn't move a step further than jist to lave the road an' lie in a dhry ditch, as I thought, to die, jist as I complated the journey to my native place! But this little girl—this goolden-haired child—kem to me, an' raised my head, an' poured a sweet draught of milk into my mouth, an' brought me food, an' sat by me, an' talked wid me, till I was at last able to join wid you! An' afther this—afther this, would you have me harm any one belongin' to her—even though he is my bitterest inimy?"

The quick changing of purpose—the sudden transitions of the Irish nature—are proverbial; and then those who had been loudest in their murmurs were loudest in their cries of approval; and a deep huzza of exultation at the magnanimity he displayed, told Dillon that he had little to fear from their opposition. So once more embracing the little girl, he gave her hand to her father, and taking the leader's arm, strode away, exclaiming:

"Whelan, you may thank your child—for 'tis she ha's saved you!"

The party all followed after him; and in a few moments more there was no trace of the scene of violence that had been partly enacted, and the brook's low bubblings, as before, alone disturbed the silence of the slumbering night.

We will not attempt to describe poor Nanny's joy at her son's making himself known, and informing her of the circumstances that had taken place—enough to say, he had managed to escape before his time was out; but as no one informed against him, he was suffered to remain in peace, and manage a small farm in the next county, where he and his mother soon after retired, as he determined totally to forsake his old mischievous pranks.

We were present at the village, altar, when Minny, who had grown up in beauty and gentleness, gave her hand to a youth—the selected one of her heart—and her gray-headed parent looked meekly on, blessing that Providence who had given him such a child. Providence who had given him such a child.

Copyright © 2023 Esprios Digital Publishing. All Rights Reserved.